Simon finds a treasure

Gilles Tibo

Tundra Books

My name is Simon and I love to look for things.

I take my telescope, I put on my helmet,
I get on my horse and ride out across the fields
to look for a treasure.

Oh! There's a sign!

An arrow points to a trail.
It must lead to a treasure.

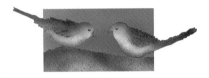

I call Marlene.
We search the field. We look for more signs.

A butterfly tries to help.
"I have a treasure," the butterfly says.
"It is hidden in the nectar of this flower.
What treasure are you looking for, Simon?"

"I don't know," I answer. "I am still looking."

Near a pond Marlene asks a turtle to help.

"I have a treasure," the turtle says,
"and it is the most wonderful in the world.
These ten eggs that will soon hatch.
What's your treasure, Simon?"

"I don't know," I answer. "I haven't found it."

At the foot of a tree we ask a squirrel to help.

"I have a treasure," the squirrel says.
"These hundred nuts I have hidden away for winter.
What treasure are you looking for, Simon?"

"I don't know," I answer. "It's still hidden."

Marlene goes home. I go on alone.

In the late afternoon at the edge of a river,
I meet an old miner.

"Look at the treasure I've found," he says.
"These thousand specks of gold dust shining in my pan.
What treasure are you looking for, Simon?"

"I'll know when I find it," I said, and go on.

At the end of the day I reach the edge of a forest.
An arrow points to the entrance of a dark cave.
This is a place where my treasure could be hidden.

I go in.

I walk a long time, deep into the cave.
I hear strange noises.
I am scared.

Suddenly a ghost appears.

"Whoo! Whoo! Whoo!" says the ghost.
"Are you looking for treasure? Let me show you mine."
A million bats fly all around me.

"What's your treasure, Simon?" the ghost asks.

I do not wait to answer. I run from the cave.

Outside it is night.
It's too dark for me to find my way home.

"Help! Help!" I cry. "I'm lost."

In the distance I hear someone calling my name:
"Simon! Simon! Simon!"

"I'm here," I call back.

My friends have come to find me.

I rush to Marlene and hug her.
I don't need to look further.
I have found my treasure.

For Alice

© 1996 Gilles Tibo

Published in Canada by Tundra Books, Toronto, Ontario M5G 2E9

Published in the United States by Tundra Books of Northern New York, Plattsburgh, N.Y. 12901

Library of Congress Catalog Number: 96-60348

Canadian Cataloguing in Publication Data

Tibo, Gilles, 1951–
[Simon et la chasse au trésor. English]
    Simon finds a treasure
Translation of: Simon et la chasse au trésor.
For children.
ISBN 0-88776-376-6 [bound]

    I. Title. II. Title: Simon et la chasse au trésor. English.

PS8589.I26S52613 1996   jC843'.54   C96-900254-8
PZ7.T52sii 1996

00 99 98 97 96   5 4 3 2 1

Canadian Cataloguing in Publication Data

Tibo, Gilles, 1951–
[Simon et la chasse au trésor. English]
    Simon finds a treasure

Translation of: Simon et la chasse au trésor.
ISBN 0-88776-388-x [pbk.]

    I. Title. II. Title: Simon et la chasse au trésor. English.

PS8589.I26S53613 1996   jC843'.54   C96-931520-1
PZ7.T52si 1996

00 99 98 97 96   5 4 3 2 1

[Issued also in French under title: Simon et la chasse au trésor ISBN 0-88776-375-8]

The publisher has applied funds from its Canada Council block grant for 1996 toward the editing and production of this book.

Printed in Hong Kong by South China Printing Co. Ltd.